Louisa in the Wings

For June and John Crebbin

RED FOX BALLET BOOKS
Little Swan
Louisa's Secret
Louisa in the Wings
A Rival for Louisa

A Red Fox Book

Published by Random House Children's Books
20 Vauxhall Bridge Road, London SW1V 2SA

A division of The Random House Group Ltd
London Melbourne Sydney Auckland
Johannesburg and agencies throughout the world

Text © Adèle Geras 1997
Illustrations © Karen Popham 1997

5 7 9 10 8 6 4

First published in Great Britain by Red Fox 1997
This Red Fox edition 2000

Printed and bound in Great Britain by Cox & Wyman

THE RANDOM HOUSE GROUP Limited Reg. No. 954009

ISBN 0 09 921842 9

RED FOX BALLET BOOKS

Louisa in the Wings

by Adèle Geras

illustrated by Karen Popham

RED FOX

JJB

Chapter One

Mum said, "Louisa Blair, I just despair!"
and I said, "You're a poet and you don't know
it!"

"Annie," Mum turned to me, "you're not
exactly helping. I thought you might have
tried to explain to Weezer why it is I can't do
what she wants me to do."

"Louisa," said Weezer. "I keep telling you to
call me that and you never do, so I don't see
why I should listen to what you're trying to tell
me."

"I *did* call you Louisa." Mum was beginning
to sound harassed. "If you remember, I said it a
couple of seconds ago. I even, according to
Annie, turned it into a poem, so a little less of
your nagging would be greatly appreciated."

"I'm not nagging," said Weezer, but of
course she was. Nagging is as natural to my
little sister as breathing. She has just turned
eight, and seems to be getting better and better

at it. I know her very well so I could imagine exactly what she was thinking. It must have been something like, "Well, being cross hasn't got me my way, so I'll try being sweet and see what Mum says," because suddenly her face was all smiley and her voice wasn't a bit whiney.

She said, "Mum, please explain why I can't go to the ballet. I promise I won't ask you again, but I just want to remind you that this will be a really wonderful chance to see almost my very favourite ballet, *Coppélia*, and it's danced by a company that comes all the way from St Petersburg. That's in Russia, and Russians are top champion dancers. That's what Mrs Posnansky told me, so it must be true."

Mum sat down next to Weezer and spoke gently. "I know all this, Louisa. Mrs Posnansky is quite right, and it *is* a wonderful company. I've never said you can't go. All I've said is, I cannot afford twenty pounds for each ticket. I couldn't let you go alone, so Annie would have to go with you, and that's forty pounds. I just can't manage it at such short notice."

"Why not?"

"Lots of reasons." Mum began to tick them off on her fingers. "Firstly, I've just paid the deposit on our summer holidays. Secondly, you're going to ballet classes twice a week now, as you wanted. Thirdly, Annie needs a whole new school uniform when she goes to Fairvale High in September, and fourthly, you used up all your savings on your new bike."

"What about Dad?" Weezer asked. "If I write and ask him, won't he send me the money?"

"Dad helps us as much as he can as it is. He has to think about his new house and family."

"I don't see why." Weezer stuck her bottom lip out and sniffed. "We came first, before his new family. He should think of us."

"He *does* think of us," I said. "He's always sending us things, and he pays for the tickets when we go and visit him, doesn't he?"

"Anyway," Mum said, "you're making me sound like some kind of ogre, who'd want to stop you going to see *Coppélia*. That's simply not true. I've said I'd pay for two gallery seats – they're only four pounds each. I really don't see why you're not happy with that."

"Because," Weezer said patiently, "sitting in the gallery is no good at all. You might as well look at the ballet on a video in the next room. All the dancers will be tiny, and I won't be able to see their feet properly or the expressions on their faces. I'd rather not go at all than have to sit in the gallery."

"Then it's not going at all, I'm afraid," Mum said. "Now come on, both of you. Help me wash up the supper dishes and then, Annie, you must go and do your homework."

"I haven't got any," I told her. "It's half-term next week, don't you remember?"

"What with your sister filling my head all afternoon, I'm quite surprised that I can remember my own name."

"I've got to write to Dad, though," I said. "I'll do it as soon as we've finished."

I couldn't understand why Weezer was so quiet all the time we were drying the dishes and putting them away. I should have guessed that she was planning something, but I didn't. I only realized later on when she came into our room while I was writing my letter.

"Have you finished, Annie?" she asked, putting her head round the door. "Is it OK to talk to you?"

"Yes," I said,

"but just sit quietly for a second while I finish this picture off for Dad."

"What's it a picture of?" Weezer asked.

"It's Brad, fast asleep. Look."

Weezer looked. "I wish I could draw lovely pictures like you," she said. "Will you let me add a little note to Dad at the bottom of your letter?"

"OK," I said. "In a minute. Just wait till I've coloured Brad in."

"Right," said Weezer, stretching out on her bed. "I didn't just come in to chat. I want to discuss something with you." As she spoke, she kept raising and lowering one leg after the other into the air, toes pointed. "It's about this money thing."

"I thought we'd finished talking about that. There's not enough money for the seats you want and that's all there is to it. I'd go for the

gallery if I were you."

"You're not me," Weezer said. "Only a ballet dancer would understand why it's so important for me to see these Russian dancers close up. Anyway, it doesn't matter about Mum not being able to afford it, because I'm going to get enough all by myself. Well, with a bit of help from you, and Tony and Tricia and Maisie."

Brad's fur was all coloured in, so I put the lid on my brown felt-tip and took out a greeny-yellowy one for his eyes. "What are you talking about?" I said.

"I'm going to earn the money."

"How?"

"I'm going to hold a Jumble Sale."

"A Jumble Sale?"

"Yes, and then I think I'll put on a dancing show. Maybe Tony can be in some of the pieces as well."

"There's no room for dancing in our lounge," I said. "You'll look pretty silly all squashed in with the furniture."

"We could move the furniture," said Weezer, looking cross.

"It still wouldn't be right. And anyway, a lot of people aren't even that keen on ballet."

"I don't care about them," she said. "They're just stupid."

"You'll care if you don't get any money because nobody comes."

Weezer thought about this for a minute and sighed. "OK, I suppose you're right. What about a puppet show? I could do it with Tricia and Maisie. We've got loads of glove puppets. You could be in it too, if you like. We'll ask for 50p per ticket."

"Thanks," I said. "I think I'll just help with scenery and things."

"OK," said Weezer. "Whatever you like. And then I shall do all sorts of odd jobs for people too."

"I don't want to wash cars," I said.

"Well, there are lots of other things we could do."

"Like what?"

"Like walking people's dogs."

"There's not much time, though," I said. "The St Petersburg Ballet are coming the week after next, and don't forget that you go to ballet class on Tuesday afternoon and Saturday morning."

Weezer snorted. "As if I'd forget about ballet class! It's OK. We don't have to go to school next week. I've made up a timetable, look."

Weezer's timetable said:

> 'Saturday: start planning everything
> Monday–Friday: do dog-walking
> Wednesday: have Jumble Sale
> Friday: have Puppet Show
> Saturday: GO AND BUY TICKETS!!!'

I said, "If you're going to put on a puppet show in a week, you'd really better get cracking writing it."

"You're a good writer, Annie." Weezer was being specially nice. "Will you help me? We could do it now, before bedtime. It doesn't have to be a *long* puppet show."

"But it has to be good if you're going to charge people money to see it."

"It'll be ace if you write it, Annie. It'll be really brilliant."

If there's one thing my sister is good at, it's getting people to do what she wants. I put my felt-tips away and got my best notebook out.

"Come on," I said. "Let's make a list of everything we have to do."

I opened the notebook and wrote 'MONEY-MAKING' at the top of a new page.

Chapter Two

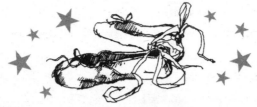

The next day was Saturday. When Weezer came back from her ballet class with Tony, she was frowning.

"I've been talking to Tony," she said. "I never realized that putting on a Puppet Show would be so fiddly. I never thought about how we're going to get everyone to come to it."

"I told you," said Tony. He almost lives at our house. He comes over every day to practise ballet with Weezer, and now he's like a sort of brother to us. He often has very good ideas. For instance, he seemed to know all about how to get people to watch our Puppet Show, and also how to get them to come to a Jumble Sale.

He said, "I'll print out something on our printer at home, and ask my dad if he'll make lots of copies for us."

"Won't he mind?" I asked.

"No, I'm sure he'll do it," Tony said.

"They've got a really good photocopier where he works. We also need tickets, but we can cut those out of ordinary paper and just write the price on them and sell them to everyone at the door."

"How many people do you think will come?" Weezer asked. "Do you think we can get twenty?"

"Twenty won't fit in your lounge," Tony said. "Maybe you should do two shows, one on Friday and one on Saturday."

"No," said Weezer. "We're going to get the tickets on Saturday. Everyone will just have to squash in, that's all. I'm going to tell the ballet class about it, so I'm sure lots of them will come."

"And I think," I said, "that we should put a note through all the letterboxes in this street asking everyone to give us their jumble."

"What about their dogs?" Weezer asked. "We'll have to knock on their doors for that, won't we?"

"I suppose so," I said. "But we'd better ask Mum about it first, to see if it's all right. I don't know how we're going to fit everything in. When are we going to rehearse the Puppet Show?"

"Have you written it?" Weezer asked.

"Not yet," I said. "You only told me about it yesterday."

"Well, if you can get it ready by Monday, then I'll invite Tricia and Maisie over for a rehearsal."

"OK," I said. "I'll go and start writing it, and you and Tony talk to Mum and then go and ask everyone about dogs and jumble. We can meet back here at suppertime and you can tell me all about it."

"No," said Weezer. "You've got to come and ask about the dogs. I can't go alone. People won't believe me on my own. They'll believe both of us. You can make it sound all grown-up and official."

"And I can't come," said Tony. "I'm going to put the advertisements on to the word-processor."

"So when am I supposed to write this play?" I asked.

"Later," said Weezer. "It won't take you long."

"All right," I said. "Let's go."

Weezer and I went from one house to another. We'd made a list with Mum of all the houses where she knew the people, and there

seemed to be lots of them. Some doors had brass knockers, others had electric bells which played a tune inside the house, and some people just had ordinary buzzer-type doorbells. I'd never realized how peculiar some of our neighbours were. Some people took ages and ages to understand what we were asking them for; others looked at us very

suspiciously, even though they must have known who we were. Lots of people thought we just wanted money to buy extra sweets with and didn't seem to believe Weezer when she explained to them about going to see *Coppélia*.

"Let's try Mrs Rosebush," she said. "They've got that pretty little dog." We didn't know what the Rosebushes' real name was, even though Mum often stopped to chat to them in the street. We called them that because they had rosebushes growing in big plant pots on either side of their front door. Weezer said this meant they were posh. I rang the doorbell, and the door opened straight away.

"Hello," I said.

"Hello, dear," said Mrs Rosebush. She was wearing a very fluffy pink jumper and her hair was very fluffy too, though it wasn't pink. "You're Mrs Blair's girls, aren't you?"

"Yes," said Weezer, "and we're trying to earn some extra money by taking dogs for walks."

"Could you do

it twice a day?" Mrs Rosebush asked. "Only I'm finding it a little difficult to get around . . .What about school?"

"It's half-term," Weezer said. I couldn't think why she'd asked me to come with her if she was going to do all the talking.

"We're charging a pound a day," I said. "That's for two walks, and we'd only be able to do it for next week, I'm afraid, because we're back at school the week after."

"That would be a great help to me," said Mrs Rosebush. "Could you come and collect Tilly at nine tomorrow?"

"Yes," I said. "Nine is fine. Thank you very much."

Weezer and I walked on to the next house. She was skipping along the pavement.

"Six pounds by Friday!" she sang. "We'll get the money in no time. We'll be rich! Maybe we'll even be able to afford a box."

By the end of the afternoon, we'd only found two more dogs who needed us, and the owners just wanted morning walks. Everyone else in our street seemed to have cats or rabbits or no pets at all. We went back to Tony's house to have a look at his advertisements.

"I've worked it out," Weezer told him, "that

the dog-walking will get us twelve pounds. That means we still need twenty-eight more. Will we be able to get that much from the Jumble Sale and Puppet Show?"

"You will after everyone sees my adverts," Tony said. "Look at this!" He put two sheets of paper on his desk. One said:

BRILLIANT PUPPET SHOW!!!
at
10 Ratcliffe Road
on
Friday February 15th
at
5.00 pm
EVERYONE WELCOME!
(Tickets at the door: 50p)

The other one said:

HAVE YOU GOT ANY JUMBLE?

We are holding a Jumble Sale
on
WEDNESDAY FEBRUARY 13TH
We will be collecting all unwanted
toys, books,
tapes, CDs, ornaments,
jewellery, scarves, etc.
on Sunday, 9th February.

The Jumble Sale will take place at
6.00 pm
on Wednesday, 13th February
at 10, Ratcliffe Road.

BRILLIANT BARGAINS FOR ALL!

"They look great!" said Weezer. "Everyone will want to come. And they'll give us tons of jumble, you'll see."

"Yes," I said. "They're lovely. But I don't think we should use 'brilliant' twice, do you, Tony?"

"What can we have instead?"

"How about 'Spectacular Puppet Show'?"

"Spectacular!" Weezer said. "Don't you think that's good, Tony?"

"OK," said Tony. "I can change it. It's easy." He sat down at the computer and started pressing buttons.

"And I'm not sure about calling it a Jumble Sale," I said.

"But is *is* a Jumble Sale!" Weezer said.

"Why don't we call it a Bring and Buy Sale?" I asked. "That sounds much more elegant."

"Does it?" She seemed uncertain. "Do you think it does, Tony?"

"Oh, yes," he said. "It definitely does."

"Right," said Weezer. "A Bring and Buy Sale, then. I'm going to phone Tricia and Maisie now and tell them all about the rehearsal on Monday."

"But I haven't written the play yet," I said.

"When are you going to do it, then?" Weezer asked. "There isn't much time."

"Now," I said. "I'm going home now, and I'll do it as quickly as I can."

"Tony and I will do some exercises while you write," said Weezer. "We haven't done enough barre work today."

They went off to dance and I started wondering what I was going to put into the Puppet Show.

PUPPETS AND things

Chapter Three

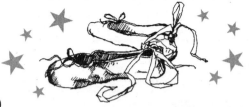

Weezer is in disgrace because of something she did at the Bring and Buy Sale. We had it in our house last night, at about six o'clock, and all the neighbours came because Tony had put one of his advertisements through lots and lots of letterboxes. We didn't make very much money because of Weezer. She was the one who said, "Everything's got to be dead cheap or no one will buy it."

In the end we only made £7.25 and that, added to the £12 from the dogwalking makes £19.25, so we still need lots more, and I'm sure we'll never get so many people coming to the Puppet Show. This is worrying me. Another thing that's worrying me is the Show itself. Every time I think of a story to write and show it to Weezer, she finds something wrong with it, and then I have to fiddle with it and fix it and show it to her again and it's all taking much longer than I thought it would. Tricia and

Maisie and Weezer all know what the characters in the story are. We've got five glove puppets:

1. *A dragon made from a green sock*
2. *A frog made of brown velvet*
3. *A knitted person called Stripy, because her body is knitted in red and blue stripes*
4. *A teddy bear called Mr Snuggly*
5. *A purple felt hippo called Horace*

It's very hard to think of a story they can all be in together, and I haven't had time to concentrate on it, because of being so busy, and because every time we have a spare moment, we seem to be walking the dogs. We only do it for twenty minutes each morning and for half an hour every afternoon. In the morning, we have three dogs (Tilly, Jess, and Pug) but only Tilly comes out with us in the afternoon. Yesterday Weezer said as we trudged around the pavements, "I never thought it would be as boring as this."

"What did you think would happen?" I said.

"I don't know . . . I thought perhaps the dogs would lead us into exciting adventures, or be naughty, or chase cats, or growl at little children. I just thought they'd do something interesting."

"Me too," I said, but the dogs were as well-behaved as could be, and trotted along quietly with Weezer and me hanging on tight to their leads, because, as Weezer put it, "We don't want them to run away. We'd never get our money if we lost the dogs."

We had also spent ages getting the Bring and Buy Sale ready.

"It's hard work, isn't it?" said Weezer. "Collecting all that stuff together. I thought it would be easy."

We had gone from house to house with a big black dustbin bag to hold all the jumble. Most people we spoke to hardly gave us anything.

"The NSPCC were collecting last week," someone said. "We gave them everything we had."

Other people said, "Well, I don't know if this will be of any use to you," and then they'd give us a lamp that didn't work, or some children's books with half the pages scribbled over in crayon, or jigsaw puzzles with some bits missing. Only Mrs Posnansky gave us anything pretty at all.

We had spread everything out on the carpet when we got home. Weezer said, "It all looks horrible. No one will want to buy this stuff. We're never going to get enough money. I think we should put in some of our own things as well."

"What things?" I said. "I don't want to sell my belongings."

"There must be something you don't want. Just have a look in your drawers. I'll go over and ask Tony too, and Mum might have some bits in the kitchen."

She went off to see them, and I was left alone to clean up the jumble we had managed to collect.

At about quarter to six last night, Weezer and I stood at the window of our front room and waited for the crowds to arrive. Brad was tiptoeing through the jumble, which was all neatly laid out on the dining-room table. He gave some ornaments a sniff, and was just starting to curl up for a nap on somebody's knitted tea-cosy when Weezer spotted him, and lifted him down to the floor.

"Sorry, Brad," she said. "You can't stay on the table. Someone might want to buy you to be their cat." Even Brad never argued with Weezer. He jumped up on to the windowsill and stared out at the street.

"Nobody's come yet," said Weezer. "Tony said he'd be here early."

"It's only just six, Weezer. Calm down,"
I said.

Mum was sitting on a chair at the front door,
waiting to let people in. "I'll do door duty for
half an hour and not a minute more," she'd told
us. "At half past six I have to start cooking
supper."

"Here they come!" Weezer shouted. "Maisie
and Tricia and Mrs Posnansky and the couple
from down the road with their little girl . . . it's
going to be all right. Oh, Annie, it really is."

She was very nearly right.

The Bring and Buy Sale was almost a great
success, except for what Weezer did. At first no
one noticed. Everyone had left and Mum,
Weezer and I were tidying up.

"We've got £12.25!" I told them. "Isn't that
brilliant!"

"Well done, girls," said Mum. "I'm proud of
you both." She turned to smile at Weezer, and
then her smile turned into a frown.

"Where's my little china vase? The one that
lives on the mantelpiece . . . I hope no one has
bought it by mistake."

"I sold it!" Weezer said. "Wasn't that clever
of me? I got five pounds for it from Mrs

Meadowes. Isn't that great?"

"You did WHAT?" Mum was so cross her face was quite white.

"Mrs Meadowes offered me five pounds for it, so I sold it to her. Five pounds, Mum. That's a fantastic amount of money. And you never

specially said you liked the vase."

"Well, I do," Mum said. "And you can just take this five-pound note and go round to Mrs Meadowes at once. Tell her you made a mistake and please could you have your mother's vase back. Go now. And I don't want to hear a single

solitary squeak out of you till that vase is back in this house. Annie, go with her please. It's too dark for her to go on her own."

On the way over to Mrs Meadowes' house, Weezer said, "We've only got £7.25 now. I don't see why Mum is making such a fuss about a silly old vase."

"She likes it," I told her. "You shouldn't have sold it, Weezer. You know you shouldn't. You wouldn't like it if someone sold your ballet shoes."

Weezer snorted. "Ballet shoes aren't at all the same thing. I *need* my ballet shoes."

"Maybe Mum needs her vase."

"What for? She never puts flowers in it, not ever. It just sits there."

"I don't know . . . Anyway, it's not that she needs it; nobody really *needs* a vase. But she likes it, so you shouldn't have sold it, and that's that. Now, this is Mrs Meadowes' house. You knock."

We got the vase back, but Mrs Meadowes made quite a fuss, and when we came back, Mum sent Weezer to our room in disgrace. I wasn't allowed in there till bedtime, so I sat at the kitchen table, putting the finishing touches to the Puppet Show, ready to show Weezer when I went upstairs.

Chapter Four

"This is all wrong!" Weezer said. "This Puppet Show is not going to work. We haven't had enough rehearsal."

"It's not our fault," said Tricia. "We came on Monday and the play wasn't ready yet."

"Then we came on Wednesday morning, and you were all busy with the Jumble Sale," said Maisie.

"Bring and Buy," Weezer sighed. "I know. We've only really been doing it since yesterday, but everyone's coming in two hours, and we're not nearly good enough yet."

"Don't worry, Weezer," Tony said. "It'll be fine. I'll be the director and tell you what you're doing wrong."

"I won't even let you watch," Weezer said, "if you call me 'Weezer'. You know what my name is."

"Oh, all right, then," said Tony, "Louisa, if you insist."

"Right," I said. "Let's start again."

Weezer, Tricia and Maisie went behind the
sofa and put their glove puppets on. I'd written
a story about a dragon who ate teddy bears for
his tea, and a teddy bear who wanted to be a
hero and kill the dragon. This teddy bear had
two friends, a frog and a hippo, who were timid
and kept playing tricks on him to stop him
from climbing into the dragon's cave. Teddy
wouldn't be stopped, and in the end he did kill
the dragon and then he got married to Stripy,
who was being a sort of knitted princess. It was
a very silly story. I'd written all sorts of bits for
people to say and even a song for Teddy to sing.
It went like this:

> "I'm going to kill the dragon,
> the dragon I'm going to kill,
> as soon as I've pulled my wagon,
> to the top of Dragon Hill."

Weezer, who was being Teddy, refused to sing it.

"We haven't got a hill," she said. "We're all up on the back of the sofa together. I'm not singing a song about a hill that isn't even there. And we haven't got a wagon. It's stupid to sing a song about stuff that's invisible. What will the audience think?"

"People," I said, "will have to use their imaginations." But I could see what she meant.

"Don't sing the song, then," I said. "In fact, don't bother with my words at all."

"You mean make it up as we go along? Are you sure? We do that at ballet sometimes. We call it 'improvisation'," Weezer said grandly.

"Try it," I said. "It couldn't be worse than it is now."

I had to admit that everything sounded much better when everyone was making up their own words. I cheered myself up by imagining myself standing at our front door and saying:

"Sorry! The Puppet Show is sold out, I'm afraid. There are no more seats left . . . Oh, you'd be willing to pay to stand at the back . . . Oh well, in that case, sir, thank you very much."

The Puppet Show was a disaster. We made four pounds. Not counting Mum and Mr and Mrs Delaney and Mrs Posnansky, only four people came who were, as Weezer put it, 'real audience'. They were Mrs Rosebush, Linda and Pam from ballet class, and Daisy from Weezer's class at school. After everyone else had gone home, we sat at the kitchen table with Tony.

"It was awful," Weezer said. "I'm never doing another Puppet Show ever."

"If we'd known how bad it was going to

be," said Tony, "we could have sold the puppets at the Bring and Buy and made a bit more money."

"Not much use having good ideas now, though, is it?" said Weezer. "The Bring and Buy Sale is over and so is the Puppet Show and we still haven't got the money we need . . . even with the boring dog-walking."

Weezer's face was looking more and more frowny, and her mouth was starting to turn down at the corners. I said, "Cheer up, Louisa." (I was careful about her name.) "Let's make a list of all the money we've got."

"We know how much money we've got," she said.

"But it looks better if you write it down," I said. I took a clean piece of paper and made a list.

- DOGWALKING   £12.00
- BRING AND BUY   £7.25
- PUPPET SHOW   £4.00

- TOTAL   £23.25

- NEEDED FOR TICKETS £40.00
- STILL TO GET   £16.75

We all stared at the figures.

"We can't go and that's that," Weezer said. "We still need more than fifteen pounds. Don't forget we need money for the bus fares as well."

"And we have to have the money by tomorrow," I said, "because that's when we're going to buy the tickets."

Weezer was looking more and more as if she was about to burst into tears. As I was wondering what to say, Mum came into the kitchen. She was carrying her purse.

"I've just been on the phone to your dad," she said. "I told him you were busy so he's ringing back later to chat to you both, but he did tell me to give you any money that you needed to make up the ticket prices. £20, is it? Or £15?"

"It's exactly £17.55, including bus fares," I said, and Mum opened the purse and put the money down in front of Weezer.

"There we are," she said. "Two front stall seats for Louisa Ballerina and her sister . . . You *shall* go to the ball, Cinders!"

Weezer jumped up and hugged Mum.

"That's brilliant, Mum," she said. "Thank you, thank you, thank you all there is! I'm so happy!" She beamed at us. "You get extra happy, don't you, when you've just been feeling miserable and then it stops?"

Tony and I both agreed that you did. I was pleased about the money, of course, and about going to the ballet, but best of all was not having to do all sorts of things like collecting jumble and writing plays for puppets which then never got used, and walking dogs. The last week had been so busy that I was quite looking forward to going back to school, where I could have a bit of a rest.

Chapter Five

Weezer spent the whole of the bus ride from our house to the theatre telling me the story of *Coppélia*. She came tearing back from her ballet class at lunchtime and could hardly eat anything at all because she was so excited.

"Have you got the money, Annie?" she kept asking me, and I kept having to get my purse out of my jacket pocket and showing her the four ten-pound notes that Mum had given me in exchange for all our odd pound coins and bits of change.

"Take care of it," Mum had said to me. "Keep your pocket zipped up and be careful of the traffic. Hold Weezer's hand crossing the road. You know she's quite capable of doing arabesques in the middle of all the cars if the mood is on her."

"I'm not stupid," Weezer had said. "I'd never do anything like that."

I said to Weezer, "Stop worrying. I won't

lose the money," and she said, "OK, I will stop worrying. I'll tell you the story of *Coppélia* instead."

So there we were on the bus and Weezer was talking, and I wasn't really listening to her properly. I was staring out of the window and pieces of the story floated into my ears from time to time.

"A spooky doctor who makes a doll . . . his name is Coppélius, so the doll's called Coppélia . . . she's so real that the hero, Fritz, falls in love with her . . . but Fritz's girlfriend, Swanilda, plays a trick on him . . . she dresses up in the doll's clothes and the Doctor thinks it's real magic and she's come alive . . . it all ends happily, though. When you see it, it'll all be much clearer. The music's lovely. Are we nearly there?"

"Yes," I said, "Come on, we're getting off now."

"Yippee!" Weezer said and everyone on the bus turned to look at us.

"I don't care," she whispered to me. "I'm going to get tickets for the ballet."

The Theatre Royal had thick red carpets in the foyer.

"There," said Weezer. "That's the Box Office."

"It looks more like a cage than a box," I said. "Look at the gold bars. The ladies who work there must feel as though they're in a zoo or something."

Weezer giggled. "We could feed them bananas through the bars."

"Ssh!" I said. "Behave yourself. I'm going to

queue up now."

We had to wait about ten minutes until it was our turn.

"Yes, dear," said the lady behind the bars. "What can I do for you?"

"I'd like two tickets for *Coppélia* for next Saturday's matinée, please," I said.

"It's sold out, I'm afraid," said the lady.

"Sold out? What does that mean?"

"We have no more tickets for the Russian Ballet left at all. Every single performance has been sold out since last week. I'm very sorry."

"Even the seats in the gallery?"

"Even those, I'm afraid. There's just nothing more available. I'm really very sorry."

Suddenly I felt cold and sick and I didn't dare to look at Weezer, but of course I had to. What would I do if she burst into tears? If she did, I knew she wouldn't stop for ages. I took a deep breath.

"Weezer," I said and then nearly bit my tongue. What a time to get my sister's name wrong! But Weezer was so unhappy that she didn't even notice.

"Don't say a word, Annie," she said to me. "I don't want to talk about it. Not ever."

She stalked out of the theatre and I ran after

her. "Wait!" I shouted. "Don't cross the road without me!"

She gave me her hand in silence and all the way home she didn't make a single sound, but sat staring down at the space between her feet, her face as stiff and white as a doll's.

She went on being silent as we walked home from the bus stop. Usually, when Weezer's miserable, I can cheer her up by chatting to her, or else I can make her laugh by telling her a joke, but I knew that she was so upset now that any words I might say to her would be the wrong ones.

Mrs Posnansky was coming out of our gate as we got to our house.

"It is my Little Swan and her sister!" she said. "I am come to invite you to my house. There is a guest there I wish for you both to meet."

Mrs Posnansky's words were like a spell. Before she'd finished speaking, Weezer had opened her mouth and begun to howl. It was just as if she'd been keeping all her sadness locked up somewhere, and Mrs Posnansky had turned a magical key. Tears poured down Weezer's cheeks. I think the noises coming out of her mouth were what's called 'wailing' in stories. I'd never heard her make these sounds before.

I didn't know what to do, but Mrs Posnansky did. She said to me, "Annie, darling, go and tell your mama you are having tea in my house. I will deal with this."

She put her arms round Weezer and led her away, still wailing and sobbing.

Mum opened our door as soon as I knocked and said, "What's happened, Annie?"

I told her everything, and I couldn't believe how calm she was about it. I expected her to want to rush off to Mrs Posnansky's and cuddle

Weezer to make her feel better, but all she did was smile mysteriously and say, "Well, that's very interesting, Annie, but Mrs Posnansky was here to invite you both to tea, so you'd better go over and keep Weezer company."

"Weezer isn't much company when she's in a state. I'll have to do all the talking on my own."

"Oh, I don't know about that," said Mum, even more mysteriously. "Go on. They'll be waiting for you."

Mrs Posnansky's house is full of lovely things to look at. She has more ornaments on her shelves than anyone I know, and lots of framed photographs hanging on her walls. Her mother was a ballet dancer, long ago, and this means that she and Weezer always have a lot to chat about. Weezer shows Mrs Posnansky every new step she learns in class, and the feathered headdress Mrs Posnansky gave her when she was a Little Swan is Weezer's most treasured possession.

"Come in, come in, Annie," Mrs Posnansky said as she opened the door. "There is someone here I wish you to meet. He is good friend of mine from the old country, from Russia. Oh, we have many, many things to talk about!"

"Where's Weezer?" I asked. "Is she all right? Is she still crying?"

"No, no," said Mrs Posnansky. "She talks with my friend. The feathers of the Little Swan are no longer in a ruffle. They are smooth and white. She is quite calm."

"How did you manage it?" I whispered. "She was so upset."

"I did nothing. It is my friend."

We walked into the lounge. There was a man with white hair sitting on the sofa. Weezer was sitting next to him, chatting away happily.

"Hello," I said. Weezer jumped up and grabbed my hand and pulled me over to the sofa.

"Annie," she said. "Oh, Annie, you'll never guess! This is Alexander Petrov. It really, really is him! It's fantastic."

I was obviously meant to know who this person was, but I'd never heard of him.

"Hello," I said, feeling rather shy. He looked just like a king. He was quite old, but his eyes were very blue and twinkly and he wore a beautiful velvet waistcoat and sat up very straight.

Mrs Posnansky saw that I didn't know who he was, because she said, "This is Sasha. I call

him this from when we were small. It is
Russian short name for Alexander. Everyone
else has to call him 'Maestro' because he is now
Big Boss."

"Oh," I said. I still didn't know who he was.

Weezer helped me. She said, "Annie, Mr Petrov is the Director of the St Petersburg Ballet Company . . . the ones who are doing *Coppélia*."

"And you are Louisa's sister, Annie," he said to me. "I am enchanted. Your sister has told me you are trying to come to *Coppélia*."

"Oh, yes," I said. "But all the tickets have gone."

I looked at Weezer to see how she would react, but she looked perfectly calm so I went on, "We're very sad about it."

"No more need for sadness," said Mr Petrov, and waved his hand in the air in a very grand way. "You come to the matinée next Saturday as my guests. You and Louisa . . . I will make very big surprise."

"Isn't it brilliant, Annie?" Weezer squeaked. "I can't wait. I'm so excited I don't think I'll be able to sleep."

She took my hands and actually began to jump for joy. I'd never seen anyone really do that before, but Weezer was doing it. It was only when Mrs Posnansky brought in a Black Forest gâteau that she quietened down and sat on the sofa again.

Chapter Six

"I expect," Weezer said, "that this is what princesses must feel like. Don't you think, Annie?"

I nodded. Weezer had certainly done her best to dress like a princess. She'd insisted on wearing her very best party dress, even though it was only lunchtime, and she'd made me put on my best clothes as well. My dress wasn't as frilly and princessy as hers was, but I still felt ridiculous wearing blue velvet just to go to the theatre. I'd said so to Weezer as we got ready. She was changing out of her leotard. The Saturday ballet class had been cancelled, and so my sister had made up for it by dancing in the lounge. She'd put on her *Coppélia* tape, and I guessed that she was pretending to be Swanilda. She wouldn't let anyone watch her, which wasn't a bit like Weezer. By the time she came up to change, I was nearly ready. I said,

"I feel a bit stupid wearing this dress."

"We have to wear our best things," Weezer said firmly. "We're the Maestro's guests. And it's a ballet, not a movie or something. And he's sending a special car for us."

"It's not really for us," I said. "It's for Mrs Posnansky. If it was just us going, I'm sure he'd have let us go on the bus."

"Still, we get to go with her, don't we?" said Weezer. "We can pretend it's our car."

"Did you hear him calling her Ninotchka?" I asked Weezer. "I bet he's in love with her."

"You think everyone's in love with everyone else. It's just stupid. He hasn't got time to be in love. He's the director of a Ballet Company."

I had to admit that it was very grand riding through town in a big, shiny black car.

"Why do you think we have to be there so early?" Weezer asked me. "It's one o'clock now and the show doesn't start till half past two. Do *you* know, Mrs Posnansky?"

"I know nothing," said Mrs Posnansky, who was wearing the same sparkly sequinned scarf that she'd worn to Weezer's Dancing Display. "Only that Sasha says we must go to stage door."

If you weren't looking for it, it would have

been easy to miss the stage door completely. It was just a dull brown wooden door down an alley that ran along the side of the theatre.

"Come," said Mrs Posnansky and opened it, looking as though she knew exactly where to go and what to do.

"Imagine," said Weezer, "if we'd been by ourselves. We'd never have dared to go in like that."

A fat, bald man was sitting just inside the door.

"We are guests of Mr Petrov," said Mrs Posnansky. "He expects, I think."

The fat man looked at a list on a clipboard. "Mrs Posnansky, Miss Louisa Blair and Miss Anna Blair."

"Anne," I said, "or Annie," but no one heard me, and I didn't really mind. I quite like Anna.

"We're on a list!" Weezer whispered. "In a real theatre. I feel like one of the dancers."

"This corridor isn't what I imagined a theatre would look like," I said.

"Why? What did you expect?"

"I don't know. Something smarter, more glamorous. A bit more like the front. I thought there would be carpets."

While Weezer and I were talking, the fat

man was speaking into a sort of telephone. He looked up at Mrs Posnansky and said, "Maestro is waiting in Dressing Room 3. That's along the corridor, down some steps, and then turn right. You can't miss it."

The corridor was very narrow. We had to press ourselves against the wall to let some people pass us. They were all wearing jeans and sweaters and trainers, but Weezer said, "Those are dancers. I can tell, just by the way they walk."

"How can you tell?" I said.

She never had time to answer, because Mrs Posnansky was knocking on the door of Dressing Room 3. The Maestro himself opened it and beamed at all of us.

"Ah, it is you, Ninotchka, my dear, and the two young ladies. Come in, come in. This is the dressing room of Sergei, who is dancing Doctor Coppélius. See, he is already partly in costume and looks like half an old man!"

Weezer's mouth was open, and her eyes were wide. Sergei stood up and bowed to us, and we could see that he was in the middle of doing his make-up and had drawn frown lines on his forehead and big black rings under his eyes.

"I am the Doctor," he said. "At your service.

See!" He picked up a wig of white hair with a plastic bald patch in the middle, and pulled it on over his own hair, which was reddish-brown. "A magical transformation."

Weezer still hadn't said anything. She was gazing at the costumes, hanging on a rail; at the mirror with light bulbs all around it; at the sticks of make-up lying on the table; at the many pairs of ballet shoes piled up beside the armchair.

"We let him dress now," said the Maestro. "There is much for us to see. Sergei will meet us on the stage."

"Are we going on the stage?" Weezer asked. "Is it allowed?"

The Maestro laughed. "If I allow it, it is allowed. But first, we meet the ladies."

We went into a huge dressing room in which about ten dancers were putting on make-up, sitting at a dressing table that took up a whole wall. Their pale mauve tutus were hanging up, ready for them to put on.

"This young lady," said the Maestro, pointing at Weezer, "wishes to be ballerina."

All the dancers smiled at us, and one of them pulled Weezer to her side. She put some blusher on her cheeks, and a little lipstick on her mouth.

"Thank you!" Weezer was breathless. "How lovely! I can't wait to see you in the show. Your tutus are so beautiful!"

"Take!" said the dancer who'd put on Weezer's make-up. "Take a flower, please!"

She took three yellow roses from a vase on the dressing-table and gave one each to Weezer and me and Mrs Posnansky. Weezer flung her arms around the dancer's neck and hugged her.

"Thank you! I wish I could be exactly like you when I grow up. Please tell me what your name is."

"Is Galina. You have heard

of famous prima ballerina, Galina Ulanova?"

"Oh yes," said Weezer. "Of course I have."

"My parents, they call me Galina after her."

"My name," said Weezer, "is Louisa."

"That is very good name for ballerina," said Galina. "Very romantic."

Weezer was practically walking on air when we left. "See?" she said. "See what Galina said? I *knew* Louisa was a good name."

"Come," said Mrs Posnansky. "I take the roses to look after them till we are at home."

We made our way behind the back-cloth, stepping carefully over cables and ropes and making sure not to bump into the backs of bits of scenery.

"This," said the Maestro, showing us a big cupboard made of painted cardboard, "is the place where the Doctor hides his doll, his Coppélia.

And this," he led us on to the stage, "is the Village Square. There," he pointed, "is the balcony of the Doctor's house."

"And here I am," said Sergei, and hobbled out on to the dimly-lit stage.

"Oh!" said Weezer. "You look so old."

"Come," said Sergei. "We will dance together."

"Me?" Weezer looked at me, then at Mrs Posnansky, then at the Maestro.

"Of course you," said Sergei. "The Maestro has told me you are dancer."

Weezer said, "I'm learning. But I know Swanilda's dance from *Coppélia*."

"Really? This you have learned already? Is very advanced."

"No," said Weezer. "I haven't learned it in class, but I've watched the video so many times. I can't do it properly, of course. I'm not allowed up on points yet."

"Let me see, please," said Sergei.

Weezer began to dance. She was never shy about dancing. You only had to ask her once and she'd begin. She didn't even need music. It was true that she *did* spend ages and ages watching her ballet videos, but I never realized that she was learning the steps as she watched.

Now she was a doll, bending her head to one side, moving her arms and legs stiffly but gracefully, bowing from the waist, turning like a clockwork toy. I remembered all over again how I felt when I saw Weezer being a Little Swan: amazed that my sister (who could be so annoying sometimes) could turn herself into all these different and wonderful shapes. It was like watching a sort of magic.

"Bravo!" said Sergei and the Maestro, and Mrs Posnansky's eyes were all glittery. Ballet always made her cry, she said, because it was so beautiful.

"We do *pas de deux* now," said Sergei, and he took Weezer's hand and they did a little dance together, with Weezer still pretending to be a doll and Sergei being Doctor Coppélius.

"Enough!" said the Maestro after a few minutes. "You, Sergei, must rest till your entrance, and ladies, you must come with me. I have to show you to your seats. Oh, very special seats I have for you today. And come, please, to my office in the interval. I have ordered ice cream, naturally.

"Goodbye, ladies, goodbye, little ballerina," said Sergei. "It was for me a great pleasure to meet you."

We all said goodbye, and Weezer stared after him as he left. Mrs Posnansky and I followed the Maestro off the stage, and it wasn't till we were in the wings that I noticed that Weezer wasn't with us. She was still standing in the middle of the stage.

"Hey!" I whispered. "Come on! You're not supposed to be on stage now."

"I'm coming," she said. "I'm coming now."

She blew a kiss to an imaginary audience and then made a very low curtsey. I knew she was hearing applause in her head. She clutched an invisible bunch of flowers to her as she ran off stage.

"Wasn't it marvellous?" she whispered to me. "I'll never forget it. Never. And listen, the orchestra is tuning up. Oh, Annie, it's just like a dream, isn't it?"

"Please to sit, Louisa," said the Maestro. "And Annie, and you, my dear Ninotchka. It is not the most comfortable chair, but you see everything."

We took our places on three small stools in the wings, hidden behind the red velvet curtains.

"We're in the wings, Annie," Weezer said just before the curtain went up. "Actually on

the stage. It's almost as if we're part of the company. Ssh! It's going to start."

The stage was suddenly bright, and a line of dancers came running into the yellow light. I noticed Galina, and turned to see if Weezer had spotted her, but my sister was sitting so still and watching so carefully that I didn't dare to break the spell.

At the end of the first act, we made our way to the Maestro's office.

"I was in the wings, Annie," Weezer said to me, "but soon I'm going to be out there on the stage. Wait and see."

"I know you will," I said, and I *did* know it. That was where Weezer belonged: in the spotlight. "Let's go and get that ice cream."